CREATURES OF CRIME

A GUIDE TO THE BAD GUYS

Adapted by Daphne Pendergrass   Illustrated by Patrick Spaziante
Based on the screenplay *Animal Instincts* written by Heath Corson
Batman created by Bob Kane with Bill Finger

Simon Spotlight
New York   London   Toronto   Sydney   New Delhi

D1456284

Based on the screenplay by Heath Corson

Copyright © 2016 DC Comics.

BATMAN and all related characters and elements © & ™ DC Comics and Warner Bros. Entertainment Inc. (s16)

SIMON SPOTLIGHT
An imprint of Simon & Schuster Children's Publishing Division
1230 Avenue of the Americas, New York, New York 10020
This Simon Spotlight edition August 2016. All rights reserved, including the right of
reproduction in whole or in part in any form. SIMON SPOTLIGHT, READY-TO-READ,
and colophon are registered trademarks of Simon & Schuster, Inc.
For information about special discounts for bulk purchases, please
contact Simon & Schuster Special Sales at 1-866-506-1949 or
business@simonandschuster.com.
Manufactured in the United States of America 0716 LAK
10 9 8 7 6 5 4 3 2 1
ISBN 978-1-4814-7837-3
ISBN 978-1-4814-7838-0 (eBook)

Welcome to Gotham City, home of Batman—the Dark Knight, the Caped Crusader, defender of the city and all who live here!

Batman stops villains—bad guys who are up to no good—but saving the day isn't always about muscle or speed! Batman studies his enemies carefully, using his files on the Batcomputer. With every fight, he learns a little more about a villain's strengths and weaknesses until he discovers how to defeat them!

CASE FILE # 36498:
THE ANIMILITIA

These are Batman's top secret files on the Animilitia—a wild team of villains led by the Penguin. With high-tech gadgets and amazing animal powers, they seem unstoppable. Can Batman and his friends bag these baddies before they take a

KILLER CROC

Killer Croc's a monster crook! He is one of Gotham City's most powerful villains; his awesome strength, steel jaw, and thick protective skin make him difficult to beat. Croc lives in the sewer system beneath Gotham City and knows the underworld like the back of his claw. With Croc's help, the Animilitia is able to sneak around Gotham City using the sewers without being seen.

STRENGTHS:
-Armor-like skin
-Steel jaw
-Mega strength
-Sneak attacks

DEFEATED BY:
-Fast moves
-Smart tricks

THE TAKEDOWN:
  Killer Croc might be strong, but he isn't very bright. Green Arrow fires a special arrow at Croc. The arrow releases knockout gas that puts Killer Croc down for the count!
  Sweet dreams, Croc!

CHEETAH

Don't let this cat out of the bag! Cheetah's powers definitely aren't "kitty" stuff. She has all the abilities her name suggests. With catlike reflexes, razor-sharp claws, and incredible speed, she's almost the *purr*-fect criminal.

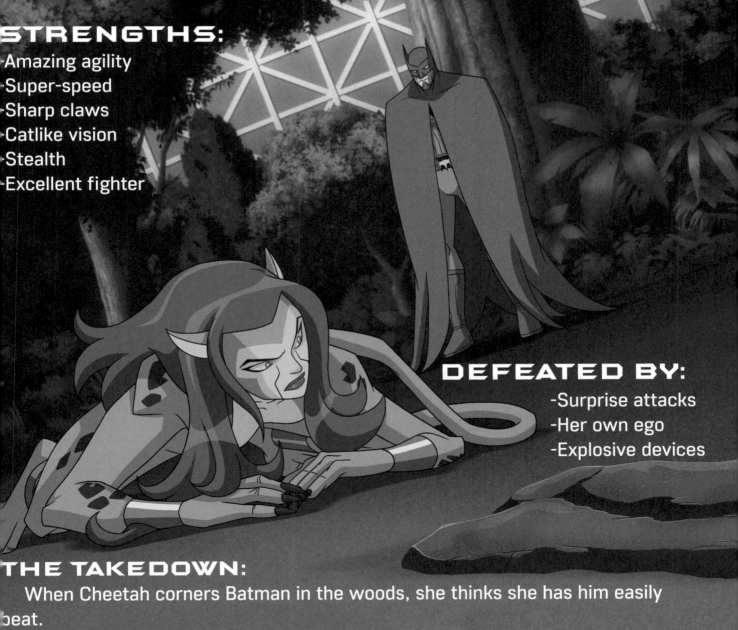

STRENGTHS:
- Amazing agility
- Super-speed
- Sharp claws
- Catlike vision
- Stealth
- Excellent fighter

DEFEATED BY:
- Surprise attacks
- Her own ego
- Explosive devices

THE TAKEDOWN:

When Cheetah corners Batman in the woods, she thinks she has him easily beat.

But Batman has a plan: He leads Cheetah on a chase through the treetops, leaving an explosive Batarang along the path. When Cheetah almost catches up, the Batarang explodes, catching her off guard!

Time to put the cat out!

SILVERBACK

Silverback is king of the concrete jungle. Little is known about this huge, mysterious gorilla with a flair for high-tech gadgets. Secretly a robot, Silverback can communicate with the Penguin's Cyber Animal Army.

STRENGTHS:

- Robot communication
- Internal computer
- Heat sensor
- Twin laser wrist guards
- Fierce strength
- Quick climber
- Gadgets galore
- Smart planning

DEFEATED BY:

- Fast moves
- Surprise attacks
- Short circuiting

THE TAKEDOWN:

Silverback's main weakness is that he loves his plans and sticks to them, no matter what. But when The Flash outsmarts Silverback at the gorilla exhibit, Silverback goes bananas—firing his laser blasters wildly at The Flash. But the Scarlet Speedster is too fast for Silverback!

That's the end of his monkey business!

MAN-BAT

Man-Bat is no joke! He is exactly what he sounds like—a man-size bat—but there's more to him than meets the eye. Beneath his monstrous exterior, he is a scientist named Dr. Kirk Langstrom, transformed by an experiment gone wrong. As Man-Bat, Dr. Langstrom forgets everything about himself and falls under the Penguin's control.

STRENGTHS:

Bat sonar
Piercing scream
Flight
Steel-snapping claws
·Strength
·Speed
·Sticky bat spit

DEFEATED BY:

-Human emotions
-An antidote that changes Man-Bat back to human form

THE TAKEDOWN:

Red Robin thinks Man-Bat will switch sides if he remembers who he really is. He's right! When Man-Bat sees Red Robin in trouble, Dr. Langstrom breaks free of the Penguin's control to save his friend. Now Man-Bat can fight alongside Batman and the other heroes.

Looks like he'll be bat-ting for the good guys from now on!

CYBER WOLF

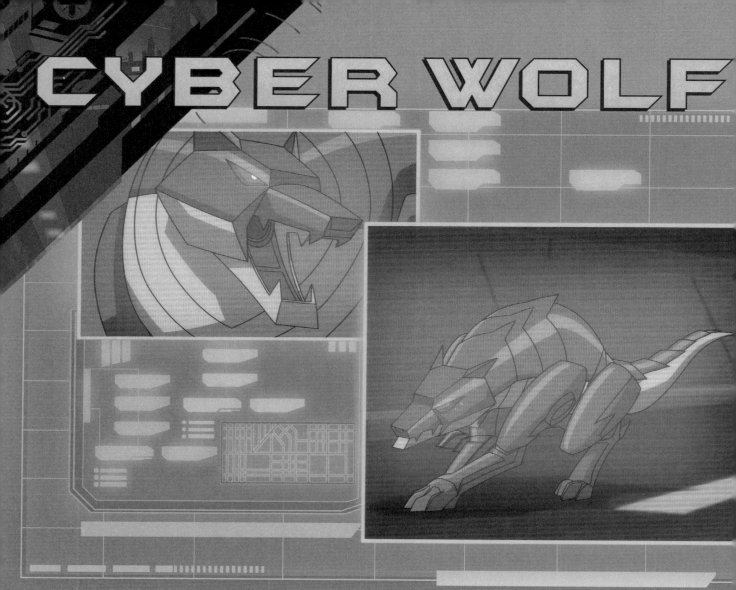

The Cyber Wolves are leaders of the pack! Built by the Penguin to do his dirty work, thousands of Cyber Wolves fill the Penguin's Cyber Animal Army. Each wolf's internal scanner helps it dodge attacks and break into laser-protected vaults. Steel cables in its back and mouth can grapple onto buildings and ledges. A Cyber Wolf can also leap from great heights.

STRENGTHS:
-Superior speed and agility
-Metal-crushing jaws
-Steel grappling wires
-Metal armor
-Internal scanner
-Ability to transform

DEFEATED BY:
-Intense force
-Electrical weapons
-Explosive devices
-Short circuiting
-Reprogramming

THE TAKEDOWN:
Batman and his allies reprogram one of the Penguin's Cyber Wolves to help them fight. The new programming makes Ace a loyal and incredibly strong pet. Ace's tail can be removed to act as a sword, and he can transform into a Wolfcycle quickly.

CYBER TIGER

These tigers will catch you by the tail! The Cyber Tigers have a similar design to the Cyber Wolves, but with a few differences. Cyber Tigers have saber teeth and tails that can rope in enemies. They are the largest of the Cyber Animals, with powerful jaws and mind-blowing speed.

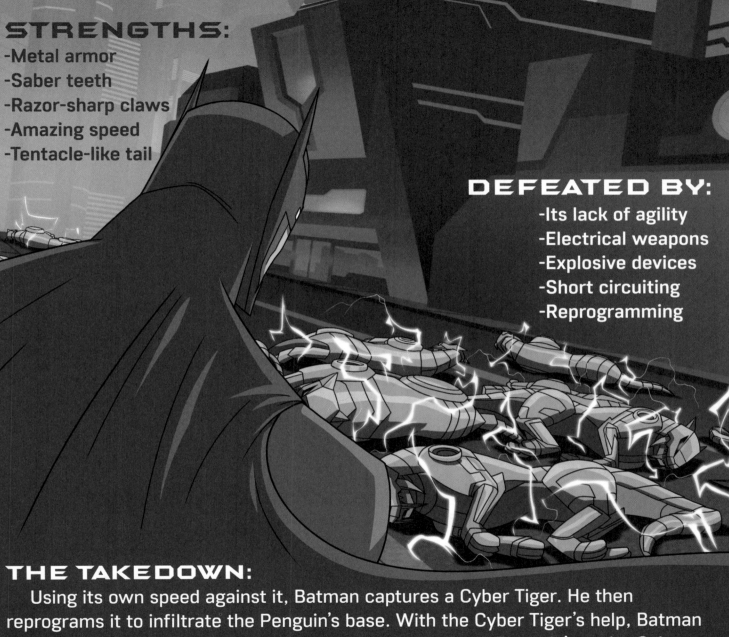

STRENGTHS:
-Metal armor
-Saber teeth
-Razor-sharp claws
-Amazing speed
-Tentacle-like tail

DEFEATED BY:
-Its lack of agility
-Electrical weapons
-Explosive devices
-Short circuiting
-Reprogramming

THE TAKEDOWN:
Using its own speed against it, Batman captures a Cyber Tiger. He then reprograms it to infiltrate the Penguin's base. With the Cyber Tiger's help, Batman and his allies unleash a computer virus that takes out the Penguin's entire Cyber Animal Army!

That's one tiger that can change its stripes.

CYBER BAT

It's Batman. It's Man-Bat! No, it's a Cyber Bat! The smallest of the Cyber Animals is the Cyber Bat, but don't let its size fool you! It still packs quite a punch. This model is the only Cyber Animal that can fly, shoot lasers, and carry heavy cargo while traveling at top speeds.

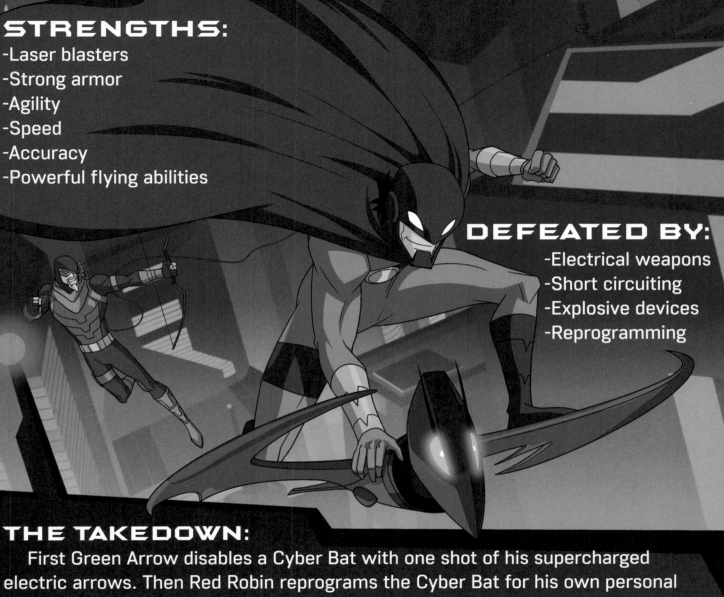

STRENGTHS:
-Laser blasters
-Strong armor
-Agility
-Speed
-Accuracy
-Powerful flying abilities

DEFEATED BY:
-Electrical weapons
-Short circuiting
-Explosive devices
-Reprogramming

THE TAKEDOWN:
First Green Arrow disables a Cyber Bat with one shot of his supercharged electric arrows. Then Red Robin reprograms the Cyber Bat for his own personal use. All heroes need a hoverboard! Quick, strong, and with an excellent defense system, the Cyber Bat makes the perfect vehicle for Red Robin.

Red Robin means it when he says, "Gotta fly!"

THE PENGUIN

Talk about squawking in the face of danger! The son of wealthy parents, Oswald Cobblepot, aka the Penguin, is the criminal mastermind behind the Animilitia. Though he isn't particularly strong or fast, the Penguin is a fierce foe. He is always one step ahead in his planning and has an army of henchmen to defend him.

STRENGTHS:
-Criminal mastermind
-Unlimited wealth and power
-High-tech gadgets
-Laser-shooting umbrella
-Secret escape pods
-Cyber Animal Army
-Henchmen

DEFEATED BY:
-Calculated attacks
-Double-crossing allies

THE TAKEDOWN:
After Batman and the other heroes shut down the Cyber Animal Army, the Penguin is a sitting duck. But he does not plot to get caught! He flees in a secret escape pod and leaves behind the Animilitia. Time to hatch a new plan!

The Penguin has flown the coop.

With the Penguin on the run, it's time to close the book on his henchmen.

The Animilitia is no match for Gotham City's smartest heroes!